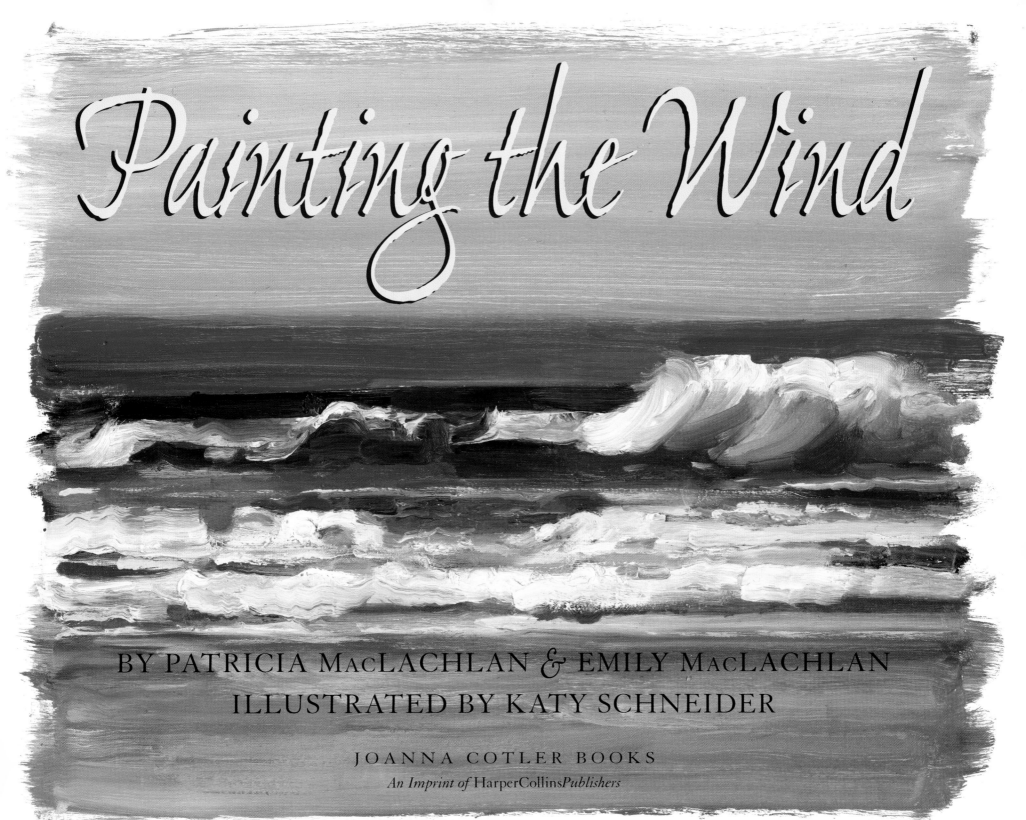

Painting the Wind

BY PATRICIA MacLACHLAN & EMILY MacLACHLAN
ILLUSTRATED BY KATY SCHNEIDER

JOANNA COTLER BOOKS
An Imprint of HarperCollinsPublishers

Painting the Wind

Text copyright © 2003 by Patricia MacLachlan and Emily MacLachlan

Illustrations copyright © 2003 by Katy Schneider

Printed in the U.S.A. All rights reserved.

www.harperchildrens.com

Library of Congress Cataloging-in-Publication Data

MacLachlan, Patricia.

Painting the wind / by Patricia MacLachlan and Emily MacLachlan ; illustrated by Katy Schneider.

p.   cm.

Summary: Several artists who paint different things, with different kinds of
paint, and at different times of the day, all paint the same island that they visit
each summer.

ISBN 0-06-029798-0—ISBN 0-06-029799-9 (library bdg.)

[1. Artists—Fiction.   2. Painting—Fiction.   3. Islands—Fiction.]
I. MacLachlan, Emily.   II. Schneider, Katy, ill.   III. Title.

PZ7.M2225 Pai 2003   2001047549

[E]—dc21

Typography by Alicia Mikles

1 2 3 4 5 6 7 8 9 10

❖

First Edition

This book is for Bob.

—P.M.

For Dean, with love

—E.M.

For Ed and Lorraine, miss you

—K.S.

I PAINT ALL WINTER LONG. And I wait.

On my island, surrounded by water and light, I paint the places where the water meets the land. I paint the deep ponds. I paint the clouds. But I cannot paint the wind. As hard as I try, I cannot paint the wind.

Then the days grow warmer. The harbor seals leave for cool waters. The marsh grasses turn green. What I have waited for all year happens.

Summer is here. And the painters come back to the island. They come on the mail boat with their paints and easels and bags of books and favorite pots and pans. Some bring their children. All of them bring their dogs.

The painters paint different things.

They paint with different paints; with watercolor, acrylics, or oil.

They paint at different times; some in the morning, some at night, some all day long.

But there is one thing they all paint.

They all paint my island.

The painter of flowers wakes at dawn when the island light first comes. He feeds his dog, Tess, and together they go out into the garden. Tess lifts her nose and smells the air.

What's there?

What has *been* there?

I set up my easel beside a clump of iris blooms gone by. The painter of flowers takes out his oil paints. He paints flowers with names like cosmos, foxglove, larkspur, poppy.

He loves the names of flowers.

Today the painter begins to paint a poppy.

He rummages through his tubes of reds. "Alizarin crimson," he says. "Terracotta, Scarlet Lake."

He loves the names of his paints, too.

He begins with a color called Cadmium Red, brushing the red across his canvas with his big brush.

The painter works for a long time, and when the sun is overhead he is surprised. We walk to the beach to eat lunch. Tess sits next to some yellow hawkweed in the sunlight. The painter smiles.

"Tomorrow I will paint the flowers in sunlight," he says.

Tomorrow he will paint his coffee-colored dog, Tess, next to the yellow hawkweed in sunlight.

"Good dog, Tess," he whispers to her. "Sweet girl."

Happy, Tess lies down and closes her eyes.

The painter of faces is late to wake.

"I sleep all night with faces in my dreams," she tells me. "And I wake with them on my walls."

Young faces, thoughtful ones, sad faces, wise faces, laughing faces; watching, wary faces. Eyes look at the painter. They seem to follow her as she coaxes her dark-eyed dogs, Emmet and Charlie, out from under the bedcovers.

The painter puts on her running shoes.

"Let's go," she says.

Charlie does not like to run. But Emmet will run anywhere anytime. Emmet is eager.

Together we run down the island road. We pass people whose faces the painter has already painted, and some faces she may one day paint.

Charlie sits, tired of running. So we walk. We walk to the only store on the island, where the painter will paint the storekeeper, Sasha, with her sweet, lined face. A sign taped near the cake mixes reads: PLEASE DO NOT EAT FROSTING FROM THE CAN.

Sasha is shy about being painted, so the painter puts Charlie on her lap, Emmet at her feet. Sasha pets them. Emmet begins to lick her feet, making her laugh so that she isn't shy anymore.

I paint a red kite hanging from the ceiling. The painter begins to paint a picture of a sweet-faced woman and two happy dogs.

The painter of still lifes has not slept all night. She painted
until dawn—the peppermint plant in the window, the glass
bowl of tulips, their green stems crisscrossing in water.
She is finishing painting the fireplace mantel crowded with
dried crabs
angel wings

a moon snail

jingle shells

smooth good-luck stones with white rings around them

a jar full of sea glass.

She yawns and stretches.

"I'll sleep soon," she says to me.

But she does not sleep. The sun comes into the room, and she begins to paint the sunlight on the old wooden floors. She paints the sparkles the dust makes after she shakes her dog Owen's blanket.

I paint a picture of a smooth gray stone.

She paints the shadows and the light, and then, when Owen rests his head on the windowsill, she paints his sad look.

"My pal," she says to him, and he looks sideways at her, the whites of his eyes showing.

"He looks embarrassed because I am talking to him."

As she paints, Owen makes a small sound.

"He's hungry," she says, still painting.

Owen sighs—a little like a snuffle—and lies down on the rag rug, waiting. He is patient. But not too patient. In a minute he will get his red bowl and bang it on the floor. The painter will laugh, and stop painting.

The painter of landscapes moves away from what he paints. He takes his dog, Meatball, in his truck with him. He has children, but he doesn't take them painting. They smudge the paintings and want to go to the store and buy things. Sometimes they whine. Meatball is quiet and good company.

The painter of landscapes paints the sky, the beach, the blue of the ocean, the black of storms. Beside him Meatball looks out at the water—two more eyes watching the world.

When it is warm the landscape painter takes water and food and Meatball, and they go out in his boat. Meatball likes the boat. He sleeps, belly up, in the sun. Sometimes he howls at herring gulls until the painter tells him to stop.

At night the landscape painter paints the moon. He loves the moon.

"So far away, so near," he says to me. When the landscape painter paints the moon he forgets who he is, he forgets his wife and children. He even forgets Meatball.

Today the landscape painter paints the beach. I set up my easel next to his. The painter begins to paint the waves crashing on the shore. Meatball runs from a wave and is caught, smiling, his ears flying in the wind, and the white of a wave blowing behind him. And that is the way the painter paints the scene: the sand, a wave, and a little rainbow of water above a running dog.

I feel the wind against my face, and I see the trees, all bent over. I pick up my paintbrush and begin to paint.

At summer's end the painters open up the doors to a barn. The dogs are outside, lying in the sun. One striped cat walks, tail up, unafraid, past them all.

The paintings are on the walls: the faces, young and old, the bowl of tulips, the full moon over a quiet sea, a red poppy that fills a canvas. The dogs are on the walls, too, caught forever by their painters. Caught forever in one single moment.

I look at the painting of Meatball running from the wave, his ears flying.

"You have painted the wind," I say to the landscape painter.

He points to my painting hung next to his, my painting of bent trees.

"You have, too," he says.

I smile. He is right. On my island, surrounded by water and light, I have done what I could not do before.

I have painted the wind.